George Sand

Lavinia

translated from the French by G. Burnham Ives

illustrations from a painting by J. B. Graff

Cover Portrait by Couture

Afterword (c) 1976 Daniel Skarry

ISBN : 0-915288-28-1

Lavinia was previously published in a limited edition by George Barrie & Son, Philadelphia.

shameless hussy press
box 424
san lorenzo, california 94580

LAVINIA

AN OLD TALE

NOTE

" Since you are to be married, Lionel, would it not be well for us to return our respective letters and pictures? It can easily be done, since chance has brought us within a short distance of each other, and, after ten years passed in different countries, we are but a few leagues apart to-day. You come sometimes to Saint-Sauveur, so I am told; I am passing only a week here. I trust, therefore, that you will be here during the week with the package which I desire. I am living in the Maison Estabanette, at the foot of the water-fall. You can send your messenger there; he will bring back to you a similar package, which I have all ready for delivery in exchange for the other."

REPLY

" MADAME:

" The package which you command me to send you is with me, sealed, and bearing your name. I ought, doubtless, to be gratified to find that you relied confidently upon my having it at hand whenever and wherever it should please you to demand it.

" But is it necessary, madame, that I should go myself to Saint-Sauveur, there to place it in the hands of a third person to be handed to you? Since you do not deem it advisable to accord me the pleasure of seeing you, will it not be simpler for me not to go to the place where you are living and expose myself to the emotion of being so near you? Would it not be better for me to entrust the package to a messenger of whom I am sure, to be taken from Bagnères to Saint-Sauveur? I await your orders in this regard; whatever they may be, madame, I will submit to them blindly."

NOTE

"I knew, Lionel, that my letters happened to be among your luggage at this moment, because my cousin Henry told me that he saw you at Bagnères, and learned that fact from you. I am very glad that Henry, who is a little inclined to prevaricate, like all gossips, did not deceive me. I asked you to bring the package to Saint-Sauveur yourself, because such documents should not be carelessly exposed to danger in mountains infested with smugglers who steal everything that falls into their hands. As I know that you are the sort of man to defend a trust valiantly, I cannot but feel perfectly safe in making you the guardian of the treasure in which I am interested. I did not suggest an interview, because I feared to make even more disagreeable the vexatious step which I have in a measure forced upon you. But since you seem to refer with regret to the possibility of an interview, I owe you that feeble compensation, and grant it with all my heart. But, as I do not wish to make you sacrifice valuable time in waiting for me, I will appoint a day, so that you may be sure to find me. Be at Saint-Sauveur, then, on the 15th, at nine in the evening. Go to my house, and send word to me by my negress. I will return at once. The package will be ready. Farewell."

Sir Lionel was disagreeably surprised by the receipt of the second note. It found him in the midst of preparing for a trip to Luchon, during which the fair Miss Ellis, his future bride, expected to be favored with his escort. It was certain to be a charming trip. At watering-places, pleasure-parties are almost always successful, because they succeed one another so rapidly that one has no time to prepare for them; because life moves swiftly, sharply, and in unexpected ways; because the constant arrival of new companions gives a flavor of improvisation to the most trivial details of a fête.

Sir Lionel was amusing himself, therefore, at the watering-places in the Pyrenees as much as it is seemly for a true Englishman to amuse himself. He was, moreover, in love to a reasonable degree with Miss Ellis's plump figure and comfortable dowry; and his desertion on the eve of so important a riding excursion—Mademoiselle Ellis had sent to Tarbes for a very handsome dapple-gray Bearnese steed, whose fine points she proposed to exhibit at the head of the cavalcade—might have a disastrous effect on his projected marriage. But Sir Lionel's position was embarrassing; he was a man of honor, and of the most scrupulous type. He went to his friend Sir Henry to lay before him this case of conscience.

But, in order to compel that jovial individual to give him his serious attention, he began by picking a quarrel with him.

" Rattle-pated gossip that you are!" he cried, as he entered the room; " it was well worth while to go to tell your cousin that her letters were travelling about with me! You never yet were able to keep a dangerous word inside your lips. You are like a brook that flows the faster the more water it receives; one of those vases, open at the ends, which embellish the statues of naiads and river-gods; the water that rushes through them doesn't stop for a moment."

"Good, Lionel, good!" cried the young man; "I like to see you in a fit of temper; it makes you poetic. At such times, you are yourself a stream, a river of metaphors, a torrent of eloquence, a reservoir of allegories."

"Oh! it's all very well to laugh!" exclaimed Lionel angrily; "we are not going to Luchon."

"We are not going! Who says so?"

"You and I are not going; I say so."

"Speak for yourself, if you please; so far as I am concerned, I am your humble servant."

"But I am not going, therefore you are not going, either. You have made a blunder, Henry, and you must repair it. You have caused me a terrible disappointment; your conscience bids you to help me to bear it. You will dine with me at Saint-Sauveur."

"May the devil fly away with me if I do!" cried Henry; "I have been madly in love since last night with the little girl from Bordeaux, at whom I laughed so heartily yesterday morning. I intend to go to Luchon, for she is going; she is going to ride my Yorkshire, and she will make your tall chestnut Margaret Ellis burst with jealousy."

"Look you, Henry," said Lionel gravely, "you are a friend of mine?"

"Of course; you know that. It's of no use to go into hysterics over our friendship just at this time. I understand that this solemn beginning is intended to impress me."

"Listen to me, Henry, I tell you; you are my friend, you rejoice in the fortunate occurrences of my life, and you would not readily forgive yourself, I am sure, for having caused me an injury, a genuine misfortune?"

"No, on my honor! But what are you talking about?"

"Well, Henry! it may be that you have caused my marriage to fall through."

"Nonsense! what folly! just because I told my cousin that you had her letters, and she asks you to return them! What influence can Lady Lavinia still have over your life, after ten years of mutual oblivion? Are you conceited enough to believe that she has never been consoled for your infidelity? Nonsense, Lionel! that is carrying remorse too far! there's no great harm done! it can be remedied, believe me——"

As he spoke, Henry nonchalantly put his hand to his cravat and glanced at the mirror; two acts which, in the venerable language of pantomime, are easy to interpret.

This lesson in modesty, from the lips of a much more conceited man than he, irritated Sir Lionel,

"I shall indulge in no reflections on Lady Lavinia's conduct," he replied, trying to express all the bitterness he felt. "No feeling of wounded vanity will ever lead me to try to blacken a woman's reputation, even though I had never loved her."

"That is precisely my case," replied Sir Henry carelessly; "I never loved her, and I never was jealous of those whom she may have treated better than me; nor have I anything to say of the virtue of my gloriously beautiful cousin Lavinia; I have never tried seriously to move her."

"You have done her that favor, Henry? She should be exceedingly grateful to you!"

"Come, come, Lionel! what are we talking about, and what did you come to say to me? You seemed yesterday to have very little regard for the memories of your early loves; you were absolutely prostrate before the radiant Ellis. To-day where are you, please? You seem unwilling to listen to reason on the subject of the past, and then you talk about going to Saint-Sauveur instead of to Luchon! Tell me, with whom are you in love? whom are you going to marry?"

"I am going to marry Miss Margaret, if it please God and you."

" Me?"

"Yes, you can save me. In the first place, read the last note your cousin has written me. Have you done it? Very good. Now, you see, I must decide between Luchon and Saint-Sauveur, between a woman to be won and a woman to be consoled."

"Stop there, impertinent!" cried Henry; "I have told you a hundred times that my cousin is as fresh as the flowers, lovely as the angels, lively as a bird, light-hearted, rosy, stylish, and coquettish; if that woman is in despair, I am content to groan all my life under the burden of a like sorrow."

"Don't expect to pique me, Henry; I am overjoyed to hear what you tell me. But in that case can you explain to me the strange caprice that leads Lady Lavinia to force a meeting upon me?"

"O you stupid fellow!" cried Henry; "don't you see that it's your own fault? Lavinia had not the slightest wish for this meeting; I am very sure of it; for when I spoke to her about you, when I asked her if her heart didn't beat fast sometimes, on the road from Bagnères to Saint-Sauveur, when a riding-party drew near, of which you might be one, she replied indifferently: 'Oh! perhaps my heart would beat faster if I should meet him!'—And the last words were deliciously emphasized by a yawn. Oh! don't bite your lip, Lionel; one of those pretty little feminine yawns, so cool and harmonious that they seem courteous and caressing, so long drawn out that they express the most absolute apathy and the most hearty indifference. But you, instead of taking advantage of this excellent disposition on her part, cannot resist the temptation to construct phrases. True to the everlasting pathos of discarded lovers, although enchanted to be one, you affect the piteous elegiac tone; you seem to bewail the impossibility of seeing her instead of telling her frankly that you are grateful beyond words."

"A man cannot say such impertinent things. How could I have foreseen that she would take seriously a few meaningless words prompted by the proprieties of the situation?"

"Oh! I know Lavinia; it's a characteristic piece of mischief."

"It's the never-failing mischief of womankind! But no; Lavinia was the sweetest and least satirical of women; I am sure that she is no more desirous of this interview than I am. Come, my dear Henry, save us both from this torture; take the package and go to Saint-Sauveur; take it upon yourself to arrange everything; make her understand that I cannot——"

"Leave Miss Ellis on the eve of your marriage, eh? That's an excellent reason to give to a rival! Impossible! you made the blunder, my dear fellow, and you must drink the cup. When a man is foolish enough to keep a woman's picture and letters for ten years, when he is giddy enough to boast of it to a chatterbox like me, when he is mad enough to be witty and sentimental in cold blood in a letter of rupture, he must submit to all the consequences. You have no right to refuse Lady Lavinia anything so long as her letters are in your hands; and whatever method of communication she may impose on you, you must submit to it so long as you have not carried out that solemn obligation. Come, Lionel! order your pony saddled and let us be off; for I will go with you. I have been a little to blame in all this, and you see that I cease to jest when it comes to repairing my mistakes. Let us go!"

Lionel had hoped that Henry would suggest some other way of helping him out of the scrape. He sat motionless, dismayed, chained to his place by a secret, involuntary impulse to resist the decrees of necessity. But he rose at last, sad, resigned, and with his arms folded across his chest. In the matter of love, Sir Lionel was an accomplished hero. If his heart had been false to more than one passion, his external conduct had never departed from the code of the *proprieties;* no woman had ever had reason to reproach him for any act at variance with that refined and generous condescension which is the most convincing sign of indifference that a well-bred man can give to an irritated woman. With the consciousness of having been scrupulously observant of these rules, the handsome Sir Lionel forgave himself for the sorrows attached to his triumphs.

"Here is a pretext!" cried Sir Henry, rising in his turn. "The coterie of our fair compatriots decides everything here. Miss Ellis and her sister Anna are the most influential powers in the council of Amazons. We must induce Margaret to postpone this excursion, which is fixed for to-morrow, for one more day. A day here is a good deal, I know; but we must obtain it, allege some serious reason for our inability to go, and start to-night for Saint-Sauveur. We shall arrive there in the afternoon; we will rest until evening; at nine o'clock, while you are together, I will have the horses saddled, and at ten o'clock —I fancy that you won't need more than an hour to exchange two packages of letters—we will mount and ride all night, reach here at sunrise, and find the fair Margaret caracoling on her noble steed, my pretty little Madame

Bernos curvetting on my Yorkshire; we will change boots and horses; and, covered with dust, dead with fatigue, consumed with love, pale and interesting, we will attend our Dulcineas over mountains and valleys. If so much zeal is not rewarded, all women must be hanged as an example. Come, are you ready?"

Lionel, overflowing with gratitude, threw himself into Henry's arms. An hour later the latter returned.

"Let us be off," he said, "everything is arranged; the Luchon excursion is postponed till the 16th; but it was hard work. Miss Ellis had some suspicions. She knows that my cousin is at Saint-Sauveur, and she has a terrible aversion for my cousin, because she knows what a fool you made of yourself for her. But I adroitly turned aside her suspicions; I said that you were horribly ill, and that I had just forced you to go to bed——"

"Great Heaven! a new freak to help to ruin my chances!"

"No, no, not at all! Dick will put a night-cap on your bolster, place it in your bed, and order three pints of herb-tea from the maid-servant. Then he will put the key of the room in his pocket, and take up his position in front of the door, with a long face and mournful eyes; and he has orders not to let any one in and to murder whoever attempts to force a passage, though it were Miss Margaret herself. Ah! here he is already making up your bed. Good! he has an excellent face; he wants to look sad and he looks idiotic. Let us go out by the gate leading into the ravine. Jack will bring our horses to the end of the valley, as if he were exercising them, and we will join him at Lonnio Bridge. Come, forward, and may the god of love protect us!"

They rode rapidly over the space that separates the two mountain chains, and did not slacken their speed until they entered the dark and narrow gorge which extends from Pierrefitte to Luz. That gorge is unquestionably one of the most characteristic and forbidding spots in the Pyrenees. Everything has a formidable look there. The mountains draw together; the banks of the Gave contract, and the river flows with a dull roar under the arches of rock and wild vines; the black sides of the cliff are covered with climbing plants, whose brilliant green fades to bluish tints in the distance, and to grayish tones near the mountain-tops. Their reflections in the rushing streams are sometimes of a limpid green, sometimes of a dull, slaty-blue, such as we see in the waters of the ocean.

Great marble bridges of a single span stretch from mountain to mountain over deep chasms. Nothing can be more imposing than the construction and the situation of those bridges, cast into space as it were, and swimming in the white, moist atmosphere which seems to fall regretfully into the ravine. The road passes from one side of the gorge to the other seven times in the space of four leagues. When our travellers crossed the seventh bridge, they saw at the bottom of the gorge, which widened almost imperceptibly before them, the charming valley of Luz, bathed in the flames of the rising sun. The mountains on both sides of the road were so high that not a single beam reached them. The water-ouzel uttered his plaintive little cry among the grasses by the stream. The cold, foaming water raised with an effort the veil of mist that lay upon it. On the higher ground a few lines of light gilded the jutting rocks, and the hanging locks of the clematis. But in the background of that rugged landscape, behind those huge black masses, as frowning and sullen as Salvator's favorite subjects, the lovely valley, bathed in sparkling dew, floated in the light and formed a sheet of gold in a frame of black marble.

" How lovely it is!" cried Henry, " and how I pity you for being in love, Lionel! You are insensible to all these sublime things; you consider that the loveliest sunbeam is not worth one of Miss Margaret Ellis's smiles."

"Confess, Henry, that Margaret is the loveliest creature in the three kingdoms."

" Yes, theoretically she is a flawless beauty. But that is just the fault I have to find with her. I would like her to be less perfect, less majestic, less classic. I should love my cousin a thousand times better if God should give me my choice between them."

" Nonsense, Henry, you don't mean what you say," said Lionel, smiling; "family pride blinds you. By the unanimous agreement of all who have eyes in their heads, Lady Lavinia's beauty is more than problematical; and I, who knew her in all the freshness of her prime, can assure you that there never was any possible comparison between them."

" Agreed; but Lavinia is so graceful and charming! her eyes are so bright, her hair so lovely, her feet so small!"

Lionel amused himself for some time combating Henry's admiration for his cousin. But, while he enjoyed extolling the beauty that he loved, a secret sentiment of self-esteem made him also enjoy listening to the praise of her whom he had formerly loved. It was a momentary impulse of vanity, nothing more; for poor Lavinia had never really reigned in his heart, which easy triumphs had spoiled very early. It is a great misfortune for a man to be thrust into a prominent position too soon. The blind admiration of the women, the foolish jealousy of vulgar rivals, are quite enough to give a false direction to an untried judgment and to corrupt an inexperienced mind."

Lionel, from having known too much of the joy of being loved, had exhausted the powers of his heart; from having exercised his passions too early in life, he had made himself forever incapable of feeling a serious passion. Beneath a handsome, manly face, beneath a youthful and vigorous expression, he concealed a heart as cold and worn out as an old man's.

" Come, Lionel, tell me why you did not marry Lavinia Buenafè, who is to-day Lady Blake through your fault? for, although I am no rigid moralist, and although I am disposed to respect in our sex the God-given privilege of doing as we please, I am unable to approve your conduct, when I reflect upon it. After courting her for two years, after compromising her as much as it is possible to compromise a young lady,—which is not a very easy thing to do in blessed Albion,—after causing her to reject some most eligible offers, you dropped her to run after an Italian singer, who certainly did not deserve the honor of inspiring such perfidy. Tell me, was not Lavinia clever and pretty? was she not the daughter of a Portuguese banker, a Jew to be sure, but very rich? was she not a good match? didn't she love you to distraction?"

" Why, my dear fellow, that is just why I complain: she loved me too much for me ever to have made her my wife. In the opinion of every man of sense, a lawful wife should be a gentle and placid helpmeet, an Englishwoman to the very depths of her being, not very susceptible to love, incapable of jealousy, fond of sleep, and sufficiently addicted to the excessive use of black tea to keep her faculties in a conjugal state. With that Portuguese girl, ardent of heart, active, accustomed from childhood to constant change of abode, to unrestrained manners, liberal ideas, and all the dangerous opinions that a woman picks up while travelling all over the world, I should have been the most miserable, if not the most ridiculous of husbands. For fifteen months I was blind to the inevitable misery that that love was brewing for me. I was so young then! I was only twenty-two; remember that, Henry, and do not condemn me. I opened my eyes at last, just when I was about to commit the signal folly of marrying a woman who was madly in love with me. I halted on the brink of the precipice, and I fled in order not to succumb to my weakness."

"Hypocrite!" said Henry, "Lavinia told me the story very differently: it seems that, long before the heartless resolution that sent you off to Italy with Rosmonda, you had already tired of the poor Jewess, and that you cruelly made her sensible of the *ennui* that overpowered you when you were with her. Oh! when Lavinia tells about that, she displays no self-conceit, I assure you; she avows her unhappiness and your cruelty with an artless modesty which I have never noticed in other women. She has a way of her own of saying: 'In a word, I bored him.'—I tell you, Lionel, if you had heard her say those words, with the accent of ingenuous melancholy that she puts into them, I'll wager that you would have felt the stings of remorse."

"Ah! have I never felt them!" cried Lionel. "That is what disgusts a man still more with a woman—all that he has to suffer on her account after he leaves her, the thousand and one annoyances caused by the haunting memory of her, the voice of bourgeois society crying for revenge and shrieking curses, the disturbed and frightened conscience, and the exceedingly gentle but exceedingly cruel reproaches which the poor abandoned creature heaps upon him through the hundred voices of rumor. I tell you, Henry, I know nothing more wearisome or more depressing than the trade of a lady-killer."

"To whom are you talking?" retorted Henry grandiloquently, with that ironical, conceited gesture which became him so well. But his companion did not deign to smile, and continued to ride on slowly, letting his reins lie on his horse's neck, and resting his wearied eyes on the charming panorama which the valley unrolled at his feet.

Luz is a small town about a mile from Saint-Sauveur. Our dandies halted there; Lionel could not be persuaded to go on to the place where Lady Lavinia was living; he took up his quarters in an inn, and threw himself on the bed, awaiting the hour fixed for the meeting.

Although the climate is very much cooler in the valley of Luz than in that of Bigorre, it was a scorching, oppressive day. Sir Lionel, stretched upon a wretched tavern bed, felt some feverish symptoms, and fell into a troubled sleep amid the buzzing of the insects that circled about his head in the burning air. His companion, being more active and less disturbed in mind, crossed the valley, paid visits all over the neighborhood, watched the riding-parties on the Gavarni road, saluted the fair dames whom he spied at their windows or on the roads, cast burning glances at the young Frenchwomen, for whom he had a decided preference, and joined Lionel again about night-fall.

"Come, up, up!" he cried, pulling aside the woollen curtains; "it is the time fixed for the meeting."

"Already?" said Lionel, who was just beginning to sleep comfortably, thanks to the cool evening air; "what time is it, Henry?"

Henry replied, with emphasis:

"At the close of the day when the Hamlet is still,
And naught but the torrent is heard upon the hill——" *

"Oh! for God's sake, spare me your quotations, Henry! I can see for myself that it is growing dark, that silence is

* Written thus, in English, in the original.

stealing over the landscape, that the voice of the torrent is louder and clearer; but Lady Lavinia doesn't expect me until nine o'clock, so I can sleep a little longer."

"No, not another minute, Lionel. We must walk to Saint-Sauveur; for I had our horses taken there this morning, and the poor creatures are tired enough now, to say nothing of what they still have to do. Come, dress yourself. Good! At ten o'clock, I will be at Lady Lavinia's door on horseback, holding your palfrey and ready to hand you your rein, exactly as our big William used to do at the theatre, when he was reduced to playing the jockey, the great man! Come, Lionel, here's your portmanteau, a white cravat, and some wax for your moustache. Patience! Oh! such negligence! such apathy! Can you think of such a thing, my dear fellow, as appearing carelessly dressed before a woman you no longer love? that would be a terrible blunder! Pray understand that you must, on the contrary, appear to the very best advantage, in order to make her realize the value of what she has lost. Come, come, brush your hair back even more carefully than if you were preparing to open the ball with Miss Margaret. Good! Let me brush your coat a bit. What! can it be that you forgot to bring a phial of essence of tuberose with which to saturate your silk handkerchief? That would be inexcusable. No, God be praised! here it is. On my word, Lionel, you are deliciously fragrant, you are magnificent; off you go. Remember that your honor is involved in causing a few tears to flow when you appear to-night, for the last time, on Lady Lavinia's horizon."

When they passed through the hamlet of Saint-Sauveur, which consists of fifty houses at the most, they were surprised to see no people of fashion in the street or at the windows. But they understood that strange circumstance when they passed the ground-floor windows of a house from which came the shrill notes of a violin, flageolet, and *tympanon*, an indigenous instrument half-way between the French tambourine and the Spanish guitar. The noise and the dust apprised our travellers that the ball had begun, and that the most fashionable members of the aristocracy of France, Spain, and England, assembled in a modest apartment, with whitewashed walls embellished with wreaths of boxwood and wild thyme, were dancing to the strains of the most infernal cacophony that ever rent mortal ears and marked time falsely.

Several groups of *bathers*, those whom a less well-filled purse or genuine ill-health deprived of the pleasure of taking an active part in the function, were crowded about the windows, casting an envious or satirical glance into the ball-room over each other's shoulders, and exchanging enthusiastic or ill-natured remarks, pending the time when the village clock should strike the hour when every convalescent must go to bed, under pain of losing the *benefit* of the mineral waters.

As our two friends passed these groups, there was a sort of oscillating movement toward the windows; and Henry, mingling with the lookers-on, overheard these words:

"That's the beautiful Jewess, Lavinia Blake, just standing up to dance. They say that she's the best dancer in Europe."

"Come, Lionel," cried the young baronet; "come, see how beautifully dressed and charming my cousin is!"

But Lionel pulled him by the arm and dragged him away from the window, angrily and impatiently, not deigning to glance in that direction.

"Come, come!" he said; "we didn't come here to watch people dance."

But he could not move on so quickly that he did not hear another remark made somewhere in his neighborhood:

" Ah! the handsome Comte de Morangy is her partner."

" Do me the favor to tell me who else is likely to be?" rejoined another voice.

" They say he has lost his head over her," observed a third by-stander. " He has already used up three horses for her, and I don't know how many jockeys."

Self-esteem is so strange a counsellor, that, thanks to it, we all find ourselves in flat contradiction with ourselves a hundred times a day. In reality, Sir Lionel was delighted to know that Lady Lavinia was placed, by a new attachment, in a situation which assured their mutual independence. And yet, the publicity of the triumph which might help that discarded woman to forget the past was a species of affront which Lionel found it difficult to swallow.

Henry, who knew the neighborhood, guided him to the end of the village, to the house in which his cousin lived. There he left him.

This house stood a little apart from the other dwellings; the mountain rose behind it, and the front windows overlooked the ravine. A few feet away, a stream fell noisily into a cleft of the rock; and the house, bathed, so to speak, in that cool, wild noise, seemed to be shaken by the falling water and on the point of plunging with it into the abyss. It was one of the most picturesque locations imaginable, and Lionel recognized in the choice the romantic and slightly eccentric nature of Lady Lavinia.

An old negress opened the door of a small salon on the ground-floor. No sooner did the light fall on her glistening, weather-beaten face, than Lionel uttered an exclamation of surprise. It was Pepa, Lavinia's old nurse, whom Lionel had seen for two years in attendance upon his beloved. As he was not on his guard against any sort of emotion, the unexpected appearance of that old woman, arousing the memory of the past, upset all his ideas for a moment. He was very near leaping on her neck, calling her *nurse*, as in his youthful, merry days, and embracing her as an old friend and faithful servant; but Pepa stepped back, observing Lionel's eagerness with an air of stupefaction. She did not recognize him.

" Alas! am I so changed?" he thought.

" I am the person whom Lady Lavinia sent for," he said in a faltering voice. " Did she not tell you?"

" Yes, yes, my lord," replied the negress; " my lady is at the ball; she told me to bring her her fan as soon as a gentleman knocked at the door. Stay here; I will go to tell her."

The old woman looked about for the fan. It was on a marble table, at Sir Lionel's hand. He took it up and gave it to the negress, and his fingers retained the perfume after she had gone out.

That perfume worked upon him like a charm; his nerves received a shock which extended to his heart and made it quiver. It was Lavinia's favorite perfume: a species of aromatic herb which grows in India, and with which her clothes and her furniture used always to be impregnated. That odor of patchouly was in itself a whole world of memories, a whole life-time of love; it was an emanation from the first woman Lionel had ever loved. A film passed over his eyes, his pulses throbbed violently; it seemed to him as if a cloud were floating in front of him, and in that cloud, a girl of sixteen, dark skinned, slender, at once lively and gentle: Lavinia the Jewess, his first love. He saw her pass, swift as a doe, skimming over the heather, riding through the game-laden preserves of her park, urging her black hackney through the swamps;

merry, ardent, and capricious as Diana Vernon, or as the jovial fairies of the Emerald Isle.

He soon felt ashamed of his weakness, when he thought of the *ennui* that had blighted that love and all the rest. He cast a sadly philosophical glance upon the ten years of positive existence which separated him from those days of pastorals and poetry; then he evoked the future, parliamentary renown, and the splendor of a political career, in the guise of Miss Margaret Ellis, whom he next evoked herself in the guise of her dowry; and finally he began to inspect the room in which he stood, glancing about with the sceptical expression of a disillusioned lover, and of a man of thirty at odds with social life.

Visitors to the watering-places in the Pyrenees live in simple lodgings; but thanks to the avalanches and torrents which wreck many houses every winter, decorations and furniture have to be replaced or restored every spring. The cottage Lavinia had hired was built of rough marble, and sheathed with resinous woods inside. The wood was painted white, and was as bright and cool as stucco. A rush mat of several colors, woven in Spain, served as a carpet. Snow-white dimity curtains reflected the moving shadows of the firs which shook their black tops in the night-wind, beneath the watery glance of the moon. Small jars of varnished olive-wood were filled with the loveliest mountain flowers. Lavinia had plucked with her own hand, in the loveliest valleys and on the loftiest peaks, the nightshade with its ruddy breast; the monk's-hood with its pale-blue petals and poisonous calyx; the pink and white sweet-william, with its delicately notched petals; the pallid soap-wort; the transparent bell-flowers, wrinkled like muslin; the purple valerian and all the wild daughters of solitude, so fresh and fragrant that the chamois fears that he may blight them by brushing against them as he runs, and the water of springs unknown to the hunter barely bends them with its careless, silent stream.

That white and perfume-laden apartment had, as if unwittingly, an air of assignation; but it seemed also the sanctuary of a pure and maidenly love. The candles shed a timid light; the flowers seemed modestly to shield their bosoms from the glare; no woman's garment, no symbol of coquetry, had been left lying on the furniture; only a bunch of withered pansies and a torn white glove lay side by side on the mantel. Lionel, obeying an uncontrollable impulse, picked up the glove and crumpled it in his hand. It was like the cold, convulsive grasp of a last farewell. He took up the odorless bouquet, gazed at it for a moment, made a bitter remark about the flowers of which it was composed, and threw it down. Had Lavinia placed it there with the purpose that it should be noticed by her former lover?

Lionel walked to the window and put aside the curtains, to divert, by looking upon the spectacle offered by nature, the emotion that was gradually stealing over him. It was a magical spectacle. The house, built on the solid rock, formed a sort of bastion to a gigantic wall of perpendicular cliffs of which the Gave bathed the base. At the right, the cataract plunged into the ravine with a loud roar; at the left, a clump of firs leaned far over the abyss; in the distance lay the valley, vaguely outlined in the white moonlight. A tall wild laurel, growing in a cleft of the rock, brushed the window-sill with its long, shiny leaves, and the breeze, rubbing them together, seemed to be whispering mysterious words.

Lavinia entered while Lionel was engrossed by this spectacle; the noise of the water-fall and the wind prevented him from hearing her. She stood behind him a few moments, occupied, doubtless, in collecting her thoughts, and perhaps asking herself if this were really the man she had loved so dearly; for, at that moment of inevitable emotion, although the situation had been planned beforehand, Lavinia fancied that she was dreaming. She could remember a time when it would have seemed impossible to her that she could see Lionel again without falling dead with grief and wrath. And now she stood there, mild and calm, perhaps indifferent.

Lionel turned instinctively and saw her. He was not expecting her, and he uttered an exclamation; then, ashamed of such a breach of the proprieties, and bewildered by the emotion that he felt, he made a violent effort to bestow upon Lady Lavinia a faultless and irreproachable salutation.

But, despite his utmost endeavors, an unforeseen embarrassment, an unconquerable agitation, paralyzed his shrewd yet frivolous wit, that tractable, obliging wit, which stood ever ready to be thrown into circulation, according to the laws of affability, and to be passed, like coin, from hand to hand, for the use of the first comer. On this occasion his rebellious wit held its peace and gazed open-mouthed at Lady Lavinia.

You see, he did not expect to find her so beautiful. He had left her quite ill and sadly changed. In those days, tears had withered her cheeks, sorrow had reduced her flesh; her eyes were dull, her hands hot and dry, and she neglected her dress. She imprudently made herself ugly then, poor Lavinia! not thinking that sorrow embellishes a woman's heart only, and that most men are quite ready to deny the existence of mind in woman, as was done at a certain council of Italian prelates.

Now, Lavinia was in all the splendor of that second beauty which comes to women who have not received incurable wounds in the heart in their first youth. She was still a pale, thin Portuguese, with a slightly bronzed skin and a somewhat sharp profile; but her expression and her manners had acquired all the grace, all the caressing charm, of a Frenchwoman's. Her dark skin was as soft as velvet, as the result of restored and unfailing health; her slender form had recovered the lithe and flexible activity of youth; her hair, which she had cut off in the old days as a sacrifice to love, now shone in all its splendor, in heavy masses over her smooth brow; her costume consisted of a gown of India muslin, and a bunch of white heather, picked in the ravine and thrust in her hair. There is no more graceful plant than the white heather; as you watched its delicate clusters waving over Lavinia's black hair, you would have said that they were clusters of living pearls. That head-dress and that simple gown were in the most exquisite taste, and the ingenious coquetry of the sex revealed itself therein by dint of concealing itself.

Never had Lionel seen Lavinia so fascinating. For an instant, he was on the point of falling at her feet and asking pardon; but the placid smile that he saw on her face restored to him the modicum of bitterness necessary to enable him to carry through the interview with every appearance of dignity.

In default of suitable words, he took from his breast a carefully sealed package, and said, in a firm voice, as he placed it on the table:

"You see, madame, that I have obeyed like a slave; may I believe that my liberty will be restored to me from to-day?"

"It seems to me," rejoined Lavinia, with a somewhat melancholy playfulness, "that your liberty has not been very tightly chained, Sir Lionel! As a matter of fact, have you remained all this time in my fetters? I confess that I had not flattered myself that such was the fact."

" Oh! madame, in heaven's name, let us not jest! Is not this a melancholy moment?"

"It is an old tradition," she replied, "a conventional *dénouement*, an inevitable climax in all love-stories. And if, when two people were writing to each other, they were thoroughly impressed with the fact that in the future they would have to wrest their letters from each other with suspicion—— But no one ever thinks of it. At twenty years, we write with a sense of the utmost security, because we have exchanged eternal oaths; we smile with pity when we think of the commonplace results of all the passions that we see dying out; we are proud to believe that we shall prove an exception to this great law of human fickleness! Noble error, blessed conceit, wherein are born the grandeur and the illusions of youth! isn't that so, Lionel?"

Lionel remained dumb with stupefaction. This sadly philosophical language, although natural enough in Lavinia's mouth, seemed to him a ghastly contradiction, for he had never seen her so: he had seen her, a weak child, abandon herself blindly to all the errors of life, yield herself trustfully to all the tempests of passion; and, when he had left her crushed with grief, he had heard her continue to protest eternal fidelity to the author of her despair.

But to hear her thus pronounce sentence of death on all the illusions of the past, was a painful and ghastly thing. That woman who survived herself, so to speak, and who was not afraid to deliver a funeral oration on her own life, was a profoundly depressing spectacle, which Lionel could not witness without a pang. He could think of nothing to say in reply. He knew better than any one all that might be said in such cases, but he had not the courage to help Lavinia to commit suicide.

As he twisted and turned the package of letters in his hand in his embarrassment, she continued:

"You know me well enough, or, better still, you remember enough about me, to be sure that I reclaim these pledges of a former attachment for none of those prudential reasons which occur to women when they cease to love. If you had any suspicion of such a thing, I need do no more to justify myself than remind you that these pledges have remained in your hands for ten years, and that I have not once thought of asking you for them. I should never have made up my mind to do it, had it not been that another woman's happiness was jeopardized by the existence of those papers."

Lionel gazed steadfastly at Lavinia, watching for the faintest indication of bitterness or chagrin produced by the thought of Margaret Ellis; but he could not detect the slightest change in her expression or her voice. Lavinia seemed to be invulnerable.

"Has this woman changed to diamond or to ice?" he asked himself.

"You are very generous," he said, in a tone which expressed both gratitude and sarcasm, "if that is your only motive."

"What other can I have, Sir Lionel? Will you kindly tell me?"

"I might presume, madame, if I were inclined to deny your generosity,—which God forbid!—that personal motives are behind your wish to recover possession of these letters and this portrait."

"It would be a little late for me to think of that," laughed Lavinia; "surely, if I should tell you that I had waited until this late day before having *personal motives*, —that was your expression,—you would feel terribly remorseful, would you not?"

"You embarrass me extremely, madame," said Lionel; and he said these words composedly, for he was on his own ground once more. He had expected reproaches, and was prepared for an attack; but he had not that advantage; the enemy instantly changed her ground.

"Come, come, my dear Lionel," she said, smiling, with a glance of genuine kindness which was entirely unfamiliar to him, who had known only the passionate side of her nature, "don't be afraid of my abusing the opportunity. Common sense has come to me with years, and I have long understood that you were not blameworthy with regard to me; I was blameworthy toward myself, toward society, and perhaps toward you; for, between two lovers as young as we were, the woman should be the man's guide. Instead of leading him astray among the paths of a false and impossible destiny, she should preserve him for the world by drawing him to her. I did not know how to do anything right; I raised innumerable obstacles in your life; I was the cause, involuntary, to be sure, but imprudent, of the prolonged shrieks of malediction that pursued you; I had the horrible agony of seeing your life threatened by avengers whom I disavowed, but who rose up against you, despite my disavowal; I was the torment of your youth and the curse of your manhood. Forgive me; I have fully expiated the wrong I did you."

Lionel proceeded from surprise to surprise. He had come there, as a defendant, to take his seat most unwillingly in the dock; and lo! he was treated as a judge, and was humbly entreated to be merciful! Lionel was born with a noble heart; the breath of worldly vanities had blighted it in its bloom. Lady Lavinia's generosity moved him the more deeply, because he was not prepared for it. Vanquished by the nobility of the character thus revealed to him, he bowed his head and bent his knee.

"I did not understand you, madame," he said to her, in an altered voice; "I did not appreciate your worth; I was unworthy of you, and I blush for it."

"Do not say so, Lionel," she rejoined, putting out her hand to raise him. "When you knew me, I was not what I am to-day. If the past could be lived again, if to-day I should receive the homage of a man occupying your position in society——"

"Hypocrite!" thought Lionel; "she is adored by the Comte de Morangy, the most fashionable of great noblemen!"

"If," she continued, modestly, "I had to decide upon the outward, public life of a man whom I loved, I should perhaps be able to add to his good-fortune, instead of destroying it."

"Is this an overture?" thought Lionel, completely bewildered.

And in his confusion he pressed Lavinia's hand fervently to his lips. At the same time, he glanced at that hand, which was remarkably white and pretty. In a woman's younger days, her hands are often red and swollen; later, they become white, grow longer, and assume more graceful proportions.

The more he looked at her and listened to her, the more surprised he was to discover newly acquired charms. Among other things, she spoke English now with extreme purity, she had retained of the foreign accent and the awkward locutions, for which Lionel had laughed at her mercilessly, only so much as was necessary to impart an elegant and charming originality to her pronunciation and her turn of phrase. It may be that the pride and timidity formerly prominent in her character were concentrated somewhere in the depths of her being; but there was no outward indication of them. Less downright, less stinging, less poetic, perhaps, than she used to be, she was far more fascinating in Lionel's eyes; she was more in accord with his ideas, more in accord with society.

How shall I tell it? After an hour's conversation, Lionel had forgotten the ten years that separated him from Lavinia, or rather he had forgotten his whole life; he fancied that he was with a strange woman, whom he loved for the first time; for the past showed him Lavinia sullen, jealous, and exacting; moreover, it showed him Lionel guilty in his own eyes; and, as Lavinia understood how painful his memories might be, she had the delicacy to touch upon them only with the utmost precaution.

They told each other the story of their lives since their separation. Lavinia questioned him concerning his new love with the impartiality of a sister; she extolled Miss Ellis's beauty, and inquired with kindly interest about her disposition and the advantages that such a marriage was likely to afford her former friend. For her own part, she told, in a disjointed, but clever and entertaining way, of her travels, her friendships, her marriage to an old nobleman, her widowhood, and the use she had since made of her wealth and her liberty. There was no little irony in all that she said; while she rendered homage to the power of reason, a little secret bitterness against that imperious power showed itself now and then, betrayed itself in the guise of badinage. But pity and indulgence were predominant in that heart, ravaged so early in life, and imparted to it a touch of grandeur which raised it above all other hearts.

More than an hour had passed. Lionel did not count the moments; he abandoned himself to his new impressions with the sudden and ephemeral ardor which is the last remaining faculty of worn-out hearts. He tried, by all possible hints, to enliven the interview by leading Lavinia to talk of the real condition of her heart; but his efforts were of no avail: the woman was quicker and more adroit than he. When he thought that he had touched a chord, he found that he had only a hair in his hand. When he hoped that he was about to grasp her moral being, and hold it fast in order to analyze it, the phantom slipped away like a breath, and fled, intangible as the air.

Suddenly they heard a violent knocking; the noise of the torrent, drowning everything, had prevented their hearing the first blows, and they were now repeated impatiently. Lady Lavinia started.

"It is Henry coming to remind me," said Sir Lionel; "but, if you will deign to grant me a few moments more, I will go to tell him to wait. May I hope to obtain that favor, madame?"

Lionel was preparing to persist obstinately in his entreaties, when Pepa entered hurriedly.

"Monsieur le Comte de Morangy insists upon coming in," she said to her mistress, in Portuguese. "He is at the door, he won't listen to a word——"

"Ah! great heaven!" cried Lavinia, ingenuously, in English; "he is so jealous! What am I to do with you, Lionel?"

Lionel stood as if struck by lightning.

"Show him in," said Lavinia, hastily, to the negress. "And do you "—to Sir Lionel—" go out on the balcony. It is a magnificent night, you can wait there five minutes, to do me a favor."

And she pushed him onto the balcony. Then she dropped the dimity curtain, and turned to the count, who entered the room at that moment.

"What is the meaning of the noise you are making?" she said, calmly. "It is a regular invasion."

" Oh! forgive me, madame!" cried Morangy; "on my knees I implore my pardon. When I saw you leave the ball suddenly with Pepa, I thought that you were ill. You have not been well these last few days, and I was so frightened ! In God's name, forgive me, Lavinia! I am a fool, a madman—but I love you so dearly that I no longer know what I am doing."

While the count was speaking, Lionel, hardly recovered from his surprise, flew into a violent rage.

" Insolent creature!" he thought, " to dare to ask me to be present at a tête-à-tête with her lover! Ah! if this is premeditated revenge, if it is a wilful insult, let them beware of me! But what folly! if I should show my anger, it would simply make her triumph. No! I will look on at the love scene with the coolness of a true philosopher."

He leaned toward the window, and ventured to enlarge, with the end of his riding-crop, the chink between the curtains. He was thus able to see and hear.

The Comte de Morangy was one of the handsomest men in France, tall and fair, with a face that was more imposing than expressive, elaborately curled and frizzled, a dandy from head to foot. His voice was soft and velvety. He lisped a little when he talked; his eyes were large, but devoid of brilliancy; his mouth fine and sneering, his hand as white as a woman's, and his foot shod with indescribable elegance. In Sir Lionel's eyes, he was the most formidable rival a man could possibly have to contend against; he was a foeman worthy of his steel, from his whiskers to his great toe.

The count spoke French, and Lavinia answered in that tongue, in which she was as proficient as in English. Another new talent ! She listened to the *red heel's* insipid speeches with singular patience. The count ventured upon two or three impassioned sentences, which seemed to Lionel to depart somewhat from the rules of good taste and dramatic propriety. Lavinia did not lose her temper; there was not even a suspicion of mockery in her smile. She urged the count to return first to the ball, saying that it would not be proper for her to return with him. But he persisted in his purpose to escort her to the door, swearing that he would not go inside until she had been there a quarter of an hour. As he spoke, he seized Lady Blake's hands, which she abandoned to him with indolent and provoking heedlessness.

Sir Lionel lost his patience.

"I am a great fool," he said to himself, at last, "to look on patiently at this mystification, when I can go away."

He walked to the end of the balcony. But there was a high balustrade, and immediately below was a ledge of rocks which bore little resemblance to a path. Nevertheless, Lionel boldly ventured to climb over the balustrade, and to walk a few steps along the ledge; but he was soon brought to a halt, for the ledge terminated abruptly at the water-fall, and even a chamois would have hesitated to go a step farther. The moon disclosed to Lionel the depth of that abyss from which only a few inches of rock separated him. He was obliged to close his eyes to overcome the vertigo that assailed him, and to crawl slowly back to the balcony. When he had succeeded in climbing over the balustrade once more, and found that frail bulwark between him and the precipice, he deemed himself the most fortunate of men, even though his rival's triumph was the price he must pay for that shelter. He had no choice but to listen to the Comte de Morangy's sentimental tirades.

"Madame," he said, "you have played with me too long. It is impossible that you should not know how I

love you, and I think it very cruel of you to treat me as if I acted on one of those fancies which are born and die in a day. My love for you is a sentiment that will endure throughout my days; and if you do not accept my consecration of my life to you, you will see, madame, that a man of the world may lose all respect for the proprieties, and throw off the sway of cold reason. Oh! do not reduce me to despair, or else beware of its effects."

"So you wish me to speak frankly, do you?" replied Lavinia. "Very well; I will do so. Do you know my story, monsieur?"

"Yes, madame; I know all. I know that a miserable wretch, whom I look upon as the lowest of men, shamefully deceived you and abandoned you. The pity which that misfortune arouses in me adds to my fervor. Only great hearts are doomed to be victims of men and of public opinion."

"But, monsieur," rejoined Lavinia, "you must know that I have been able to profit by the stern lessons of my destiny; that I am on my guard to-day against my own heart and against another's. I know that it is not always in a man's power to keep his oaths, and that whatever he obtains he misuses. That being so, monsieur, do not hope to move me. If you are speaking seriously, here is my reply: I am invulnerable. This woman who has been so decried for her youthful errors, is surrounded henceforth by a stouter rampart than virtue—distrust."

"Ah! I see that you do not understand me, madame," cried the count, falling on his knees. "May I be accursed if I have ever had a thought of presuming upon your misfortunes, to hope for sacrifices which your pride condemns."

"Are you perfectly sure that you have never had such a thought?" said Lavinia, with her sad smile.

"Well, I will be frank," said Monsieur de Morangy, with an accent of truth in which the mannerisms of the great nobleman vanished entirely. "Perhaps I may have had, before I knew you, the thought which I spurn now with profound remorse. In your presence, feigning is impossible, Lavinia; you subdue the will, you reduce cunning to naught, you command veneration. Oh! since I have known what you are, I swear that my adoration has been worthy of you. Listen to me, madame, and let me await my sentence at your feet. I desire to devote my whole future to you by oaths that cannot be broken. It is an honorable name, I venture to believe, and a handsome fortune, of which, as you are aware, I am not vain, that I lay at your feet, as well as a heart that adores you, a heart that beats for you alone."

"So you really mean to offer me marriage?" said Lady Lavinia, without, however, exhibiting offensive surprise. "I thank you, monsieur, for this proof of esteem and attachment."

And she offered him her hand with much warmth.

"God of mercy! she accepts!" cried the count, covering that hand with kisses.

"No, monsieur," said Lavinia; "I ask you to give me time for reflection."

"Alas! but may I hope?"

"I do not know; rely, at all events, upon my gratitude. Adieu. Go back to the ball; I insist upon it. I will be there in an instant."

The count passionately kissed the hem of her cape, and left the room. As soon as he had closed the door, Lionel put aside the curtain, ready to receive permission from Lady Blake to return. But she was sitting on the sofa, with her back to the window. Lionel could see her face reflected in the mirror opposite them. Her eyes were fixed on the floor, her attitude dejected and thoughtful. Buried in absorbing meditation, she had completely forgotten Lionel, and the exclamation of surprise that escaped her when he suddenly appeared in the room was an ingenuous avowal of that painful absorption.

He was pale with anger; but he restrained himself.

"You must agree," he said to her, "that I respected your new attachment, madame. It required the most profound disinterestedness to listen to insulting remarks about myself, purposely provoked, perhaps,—and to remain quietly in my hiding-place."

"Purposely?" repeated Lavinia, gazing sternly at him. "How dare you think so of me, monsieur? If you entertain such ideas, go!"

"No, no; I do not think so," said Lionel, walking toward her, and grasping her arm excitedly. "Pay no heed to what I say. I am very much disturbed.—You surely must have relied upon my strength of mind, to force me to witness such a scene."

"On your strength of mind, Lionel? I don't understand that phrase. You mean, do you not, that I counted upon your indifference?"

"Laugh at me as much as you choose; be pitiless, trample on me! you have the right to do it. But I am very unhappy!"

He was deeply moved. Lavinia believed, or pretended to believe, that he was acting a part.

"Let us have done with this," she said, rising. "You should have taken advantage of the reply you heard me make just now to the Comte de Morangy; and yet that man's love does not offend me.—Farewell, Lionel! Let us part forever, but not in bitterness of spirit. Here are your letters and your portrait. Come, release my hand; I must return to the ball."

"You must return to dance with Monsieur de Morangy, I suppose?" said Lionel, dashing his picture angrily on the floor, and grinding it under his heel.

"Listen," said Lavinia, slightly pale, but calm; "the Comte de Morangy offers me high rank and complete rehabilitation in society. My marriage to an elderly nobleman never cleansed me completely from the cruel stain that disfigures an abandoned woman. Every one knows that an old man always receives more than he gives. But a wealthy, noble young man, envied by all, loved by the women,—that is a very different matter! That deserves consideration, Lionel; and I am very glad that I have handled the count carefully thus far. I divined long ago the honesty of his intentions."

"O woman! vanity never dies in you!" exclaimed Lionel angrily, when she had gone.

He joined Henry at the inn. His friend was awaiting him impatiently.

"The devil take you, Lionel!" he cried. "Here have I been waiting in my stirrups a good hour for you! Think of it! two hours for an interview of this sort! Come, off we go! you can tell me about it on the road."

"Good-night, Henry. Go, tell Miss Margaret that the bolster lying in my bed is at death's door. I remain here."

"Heavens and earth! what do you say?" cried Henry; "you don't mean to go to Luchon?"

"I will go some other time; I shall remain here now."

"Why, you are dreaming, man! It isn't possible! You can't have made it up with Lady Blake?"

"No, not so far as I know; far from it! But I am tired and out of sorts, lame all over; I am going to remain here."

Henry fell from the clouds. He exhausted all his eloquence to induce Lionel to go; but, failing utterly, he dismounted, and tossed his bridle to the hostler.

"Well, if you are determined, I will also stay," he exclaimed. "It seems to me such a good joke, that I propose to see it through to the end. To the devil with love-affairs at Bagnères, and the plans we made on the road! My excellent friend Sir Lionel Bridgemont is giving a performance for my benefit; I will be an attentive and absorbed witness of his drama."

Lionel would have given all the world to be rid of this irresponsible, bantering spy upon his actions; but it was impossible.

"As you are determined to follow me," he said, "I warn you that I am going to the ball."

"To the ball? very good. Dancing is an excellent remedy for the spleen and lameness."

Lavinia was dancing with Monsieur de Morangy. Lionel had never seen her dance. When she had come to England, she knew nothing but the *bolero*, and she had never ventured to dance it under the austere skies of Great Britain. Since then, she had learned our contradances, and she displayed in them the voluptuous grace of the Spaniard combined with an indefinable touch of English prudery, which tempered its exuberance. People stood on the benches to watch her dance. The Comte de Morangy was triumphant. Lionel was lost in the crowd.

There is so much vanity in the heart of man! Lionel suffered bitterly to see her who was long swayed and imprisoned by her love for him, who was once his alone, and whom the world would not have dared to come to take from his arms, now free and proud, encompassed by homage, and finding in every glance revenge or reparation for the past. When she returned to her place, Lionel—the count's attention being distracted for a moment—glided adroitly to her side, and picked up her fan,

which she had just dropped. Lavinia did not expect to
see him there. A feeble cry escaped her, and her face
turned perceptibly pale.

"Ah! great heaven!" she exclaimed; "I thought that
you were on the road to Bagnères."

"Have no fear, madame," he said, in an undertone;
"I will not compromise you with the Comte de Morangy."

However, he could not restrain himself for long, but
soon returned and asked her to dance.

She accepted his invitation.

"Must I not ask Monsieur le Comte de Morangy's
permission also?" he asked.

The ball lasted until daybreak; Lady Lavinia was sure
of making such functions last as long as she remained.
Under cover of the confusion which always creeps into
the most orderly festivity as the night advances, Lionel
was able to speak with her frequently. That night completely turned his head. Intoxicated by the charms of
Lady Blake, spurred on by the rivalry of the count, irritated by the homage of the crowd, which constantly
thrust itself between him and her, he strove with all
his power to rekindle that extinct passion, and self-esteem
made its spur felt so sharply that he left the ball in a state
of indescribable excitement.

He tried in vain to sleep. Henry, who had paid court
to all the women, and danced all the contradances, snored
lustily. As soon as he awoke, and while rubbing his eyes,
he said:

"Well, Lionel, God save us, my dear fellow! this is a
very entertaining episode, this reconciliation between you
and my cousin; for you need not hope to deceive me,
I know the secret now. When we entered the ballroom,
Lavinia was sad, and dancing with an absent-minded air;
as soon as she saw you, her eyes lighted up, her brow

cleared. She was radiant during the waltz, when you whirled her through the crowd like a feather. Lucky Lionel! a lovely fiancée and a fine dowry at Luchon, a lovely mistress and a grand triumph at Saint-Sauveur!"

"A truce to your nonsense!" said Lionel, angrily.

Henry was dressed first. He went out to see what was going on, and soon returned, making his accustomed uproar on the staircase.

"Alas! Henry," said his friend, "will you never lose that gasping voice and that frantic gesticulation? You always act as if you had just started a hare, and as if you took the people you were talking to for uncoupled hounds."

"To horse! to horse!" cried Henry. "Lady Lavinia Blake is in the saddle; she is about starting for Gèdres with ten other young madcaps and Heaven knows how many beaux, the Comte de Morangy at their head—which does not mean that she has not the Comte de Morangy in her head, be it understood!"

"Silence, *clown!*" cried Lionel. "To horse, as you say, and let us be off!"

The riding-party had the start of them. The road to Gèdres is a steep path, a sort of staircase cut in the rock, skirting the precipice, presenting innumerable obstacles to horses, innumerable real dangers to their riders. Lionel started off at a gallop. Henry thought that he was mad; but, considering that his honor was involved in not being left behind, he rode after him. Their arrival created a strange effect on the caravan. Lavinia shuddered at sight of those two reckless creatures riding along the edge of a frightful abyss. When she recognized Lionel and her cousin, she turned pale and nearly fell from her horse. The Comte de Morangy noticed it, and did not take his eyes from her face. He was jealous.

His jealousy acted as an additional spur to Lionel.
Throughout the day, he fought obstinately for Lavinia's
slightest glance. The difficulty of speaking to her, the
excitement of the ride, the emotions aroused by the sublime spectacle of the region through which they rode,
the clever and always good-humored resistance of Lady
Blake, her skill in managing her horse, her courage, her
grace, the words, always natural and always poetic, in
which she described her sensations,—all combined to stir
Sir Lionel to the depths of his being. It was a very
fatiguing day for the poor woman, beset by two lovers
between whom she tried to hold the scales even; so that
she accorded a grateful welcome to her jovial cousin and
his noisy nonsense, when he spurred his horse between
her and her adorers.

At nightfall, the sky was covered with clouds. A severe
storm seemed imminent. The riders quickened their pace,
but they were still more than a league from Saint-Sauveur
when the storm burst. It grew very dark; the horses
were frightened, and the Comte de Morangy's ran away
with him. The little cavalcade became scattered, and
the utmost efforts of the guides, who accompanied them
on foot, were required to prevent some serious accident
from bringing to a melancholy close a day that had begun
so merrily.

Lionel, lost in the appalling darkness, compelled to walk
along the edge of the cliff, leading his horse, for fear of
falling over the precipice with him, was tormented by the
keenest disquietude. He had lost sight of Lavinia, despite
all his efforts, and had been seeking her anxiously for
fifteen minutes, when a flash of lightning revealed the
figure of a woman seated on a rock just above the road.
He stopped, listened, and recognized Lady Blake's voice;
but a man was with her; it could be no one but Monsieur

de Morangy. Lionel cursed him in his heart; and, bent upon disturbing his rival's happiness, if he could do no more, he walked toward the couple as best he could. What was his joy on recognizing Henry with his cousin! He, like the kind-hearted, devil-may-care comrade he was, gave up his place to him, and walked away to hold the horses.

Nothing is so solemn and magnificent as the tumult of a storm in the mountains. The loud voice of the thunder, rumbling over the chasms, is repeated and echoes loudly in their depths; the wind, lashing the tall fir-trees and forcing them against the perpendicular cliff as a garment clings to the human form, also plunges into the gorges and utters shrill, long-drawn laments like sobs. Lavinia, absorbed in contemplation of the imposing spectacle, listened to the numberless noises of the storm-riven mountain, waiting until another flash should cast its bluish glare over the landscape. She started when it showed her Sir Lionel seated by her side, in the place occupied by her cousin a moment before. Lionel thought that she was frightened by the storm, and he took her hand to reassure her. Another flash showed her to him, with one elbow resting on her knee, and her chin on her hand, gazing enthusiastically at the wonderful scene produced by the raging elements. "Great heaven!" she exclaimed; "how beautiful it is! how dazzling and soft at once that blue glare! Did you see the jagged edges of the rock that gleamed like sapphires, and that livid background against which the ice-clad peaks towered aloft like giant spectres in their shrouds? Did you notice, too, that, in the sudden passage from darkness to light and from light to darkness, everything seemed to move and waver, as if the mountains were tottering to their fall?"

"I see nothing but you, Lavinia," he said, vehemently;

"I hear no voice but yours, I breathe no air but your breath, I have no emotion except that of feeling that you are near me. Do you know that I love you madly? Yes, you know it; you must have seen it to-day, and perhaps you wanted it to be so. Very well! if that is so, enjoy your triumph. I am at your feet, I ask you to forgive me and to forget the past,—I ask it with my face in the dust; I ask you to give me the future, oh! I ask it with passionate fervor, and you must grant my request, Lavinia; for I want you with all my heart, and I have rights over you——"

"Rights?" she repeated, withdrawing her hand.

"Does not the wrong I did you give me a right, a ghastly right, Lavinia? And if you allowed me to assume it in order to ruin your life, can you take it from me to-day, when I seek to claim it anew and to repair my crimes?"

We know all that a man can say under such circumstances. Lionel was more eloquent than I should have been in his place. He became strangely excited; and, despairing of his ability to overcome Lady Blake's resistance in any other way, seeing, moreover, that by making a less complete submission than his rival he gave him a very valuable advantage, he rose to the same level of devotion: he offered Lavinia his name and his fortune.

"Can you dream of such a thing?" she said, with emotion. "You would abandon Miss Ellis, when she is betrothed to you, when your marriage is already appointed?"

"I will do it," he replied. "I will do what the world will call insulting and criminal. Perhaps I shall have to atone for it with my blood; but I am ready to do anything to obtain you; for the greatest crime of my life is my failure to appreciate you, and my first duty, to return to you. Oh! speak, Lavinia! give me back the happiness I lost when I lost you. To-day, I shall know how to appreciate and retain it; for I, too, have changed: I am no longer the ambitious, restless man whom an unknown future tormented with its deceitful promises. I know life to-day, I know what the world and its false splendor are worth. I know that not one of my triumphs was worth a single glance from you; and the chimera of happiness I have pursued, has always avoided me until this day, when it leads me back to you. Oh! Lavinia, do you, too, come back to me! Who will love you as I will? who will see, as I see, the grandeur, patience, and pity that your heart contains?"

Lavinia did not speak, but her heart beat with a violence which Lionel detected. Her hand trembled in his, and she did not try to withdraw it, nor a lock of hair which the wind had loosened and which Lionel covered with kisses. They did not feel the rain, which was falling in large but infrequent drops. The wind had diminished, the sky became somewhat lighter, and the Comte de Morangy came toward them as quickly as his lame and shoeless horse, which had nearly killed him by falling over a rock, could bring him.

Lavinia perceived him at last, and abruptly tore herself away from Lionel's caresses. Lionel, furious at the interruption, but full of love and hope, assisted her to remount, and escorted her to her door. There she said to him, lowering her voice:

"Lionel, you have made me an offer of which I realize the full value. I cannot reply without mature reflection."

"O God! that is the same reply you gave Monsieur de Morangy!"

"No, no; it is not the same thing," she replied, in an altered voice. "But your presence here may give rise

to many absurd reports. If you really love me, Lionel,
you will swear to obey me."

"I swear it by God and by you."

"Very well! go away at once, and return to Bagnères;
on my part, I promise you that you shall have my reply
within forty hours."

"But what will become of me, great God! during that
century of suspense?"

"You will hope," said Lavinia, hurriedly closing the
door, as if she were afraid of saying too much.

Lionel did hope. His reasons for hoping were a word
from Lavinia and all the arguments of his own self-
esteem.

"You are wrong to abandon the game," said Henry, as
they rode away; "Lavinia was beginning to melt. On
my word, Lionel, that doesn't seem like you. Even if
for no other reason than not to leave Morangy master of
the field—— But I see that you are more in love with
Miss Ellis than I thought."

Lionel was too preoccupied to listen to him. He passed
the interval fixed by Lavinia, locked in his room, repre-
senting that he was ill; and did not deign to confide in
Sir Henry, who lost himself in conjectures concerning his
conduct. At last the letter arrived; it was in these terms:

"*Neither the one nor the other!* When you receive
this letter, when Monsieur de Morangy, whom I have
sent to Tarbes, receives his reply, I shall be far from you
both; I shall have gone, gone forever, gone irrevocably,
so far as you and he are concerned.

"You offer me name and rank and fortune; you believe
that a brilliant position in society has a great fascination
for a woman. Oh, no! not for her who knows society
and despises it as I do. Do not think, however, Lionel,

that I disdain the offer you made to sacrifice a brilliant marriage, and bind yourself to me forever.

"You realized what a cruel blow it is to a woman's self-esteem to be abandoned, what a glorious triumph it is to bring back a once faithless swain to her feet, and you thought to compensate me by that triumph for all I have suffered; so I give you my esteem once more, and I would forgive you the past had I not done so long ago.

"But understand, Lionel, that it is not in your power to repair the wrong. No, it is in no man's power. The blow I received was a deadly blow; it killed the power to love in me forever; it extinguished the torch of illusions, and life appears to me in a dull and miserable light.

"But I do not complain of my destiny; it was bound to come, sooner or later. We all live to grow old, and to see all our joys overshadowed by disappointments. My disillusionment came when I was rather young, to be sure, and the craving for love survived for a long while the faculty of having faith in man. I have struggled long and often against my youth, as against a desperate foe; I have always succeeded in beating it.

"And do you imagine that this last struggle against you, this resistance to the promises you have made, is not exceedingly hard and painful? I may confess it, now that flight has placed me beyond all danger of surrender: I love you still, I feel it; the imprint of the first object of one's love is never entirely effaced; it seems to have vanished; we fall asleep, oblivious of the pain we have suffered; but let the image of the past arise, let the old idol reappear, and we are ready to bend the knee as before. Oh! fly, fly, phantom and falsehood! you are but a shadow, and if I should venture to follow you, you would lead me again among the reefs, and leave me there shattered and dying. Fly! I no longer believe in you.

I know that you cannot arrange the future as you will, and that, though your lips may be sincere to-day, the frailty of your heart will force you to lie to-morrow.

"And why should I blame you for being like that? are we not all weak and fickle? Was I not myself calm and cold when I approached you yesterday? Was I not perfectly certain that I could not love you? Had I not encouraged the Comte de Morangy's suit? And yet, in the evening, when you sat beside me on that rock, when you spoke to me in such an impassioned tone, amid the wind and the storm, did I not feel my heart soften and melt? Ah! now that I reflect, I know that it was your voice of the old days, your passion of the old days, you, my first love, my youth, that came back to me all at once, for a moment!

"And now, when my blood is cool, I feel a deathly depression; for I am awake, and I remember that I dreamed a lovely dream in the midst of a melancholy life.

"Farewell, Lionel! Assuming that your desire to marry me should last until the moment of its fulfilment (and even now, perhaps, you are beginning to feel that I may be right in refusing you), you would have been unhappy in the constraint imposed by such a bond; you would have found that the world—always ungrateful and sparing of praise for our good deeds—would look upon yours as the performance of a duty, and would deny you the triumph which perhaps you would expect. Then you would have thrown away self-content, and have failed to obtain the admiration upon which you counted. Who knows! perhaps I myself should have forgotten too quickly all that was noble in your return to me, and have accepted your new love as a reparation due to your honor. Oh! let us not mar the hour of honest impulse and mutual confidence we enjoyed last night; let us remember it always, but never seek to repeat it.

"Have no fear for your self-esteem so far as the Comte de Morangy is concerned; I have never loved him. He is one of the innumerable weak creatures who have failed—even with my assistance, alas!—to make my dead heart beat again. I would not even want him for a husband. A man of his rank always sells too dear the protection he bestows, by always making it felt. And then, I detest marriage, I detest all men, I detest everlasting pledges, promises, plans, the arranging of the future, in advance, by contracts and bargains at which Destiny always snaps its fingers. I no longer care for anything but travel, reverie, solitude, the uproar of the world, to walk through it and laugh at it, and poetry to endure the past, and God to give me hope for the future."

Sir Lionel Bridgemont's self-esteem was deeply mortified at first; for, to console those readers who may have become too warmly interested in him, we must say that in forty hours he had reflected seriously. In the first place, he thought of taking horse, following Lady Blake, overcoming her resistance, and triumphing over her cold common sense. Then he thought that she might persist in her refusal, and that, meanwhile, Miss Ellis might take offence at his conduct, and break off the match.—He remained.

"Well," said Henry to him, the next day, when he saw him kiss Miss Margaret's hand, who bestowed that mark of forgiveness on him, after a sharp quarrel concerning his absence; "next year, we will enter Parliament."

Afterword

Lavinia is the second in Shameless Hussy's George Sand reprint series. The first was *The Haunted Pool*, a pastoral novel written to capture French peasant life; to record them as they had not recorded themselves. *The Snowman* is being serialized in Shameless Hussy Review.

Lavinia is a novel of an entirely different type from either of the above - concise, witty, worldly - a novel of manners with a central character who can only remind us of Sand herself. It describes the life she knew best, the world in which she moved, & the set of social values she supported & flaunted.

This is the novel of a woman who flaunts. A strong, seasoned woman who has learned to discount the words & feelings of the men around her. *Lavinia* is a feminist document. It effaces the image of the perpetual heroine in travail, who by just-plain-goodness & luck outwaits a world of terrible people. Not a saint, but certainly a central character, Lavinia spurns both a marriage with the man who once abandoned her, & with an overbearing count, saying: "I detest all marriage, I detest all men, I detest everlasting pledges, promises, plans, the arranging of the future in advance by contracts & bargains at which Destiny always snaps its fingers."

Daniel Skarry
December 6, 1976
Shameless Hussy Press